Pay Attention, Slosh!

Mark Smith • illustrated by Gail Piazza

Albert Whitman & Company • Morton Grove, Illinois

Library of Congress Cataloging-in-Publication Data

Smith, Mark.
Pay attention, Slosh! / written by Mark Smith ; illustrated by Gail Piazza.
p.   cm.
Summary: Eight-year-old Josh hates being unable to concentrate or control himself,
but with the help of his parents, his teacher, and a doctor, he learns to deal with
his condition, known as ADHD or attention-deficit hyperactivity disorder.
ISBN 0-8075-6378-1
[1. Attention-deficit hyperactivity disorder—Fiction. 2. Learning disabilities—Fiction.]
I. Piazza, Gail, 1955-   ill. II. Title.
PZ7.S65496Pay 1997
[Fic]—dc21
97-6154
CIP
AC

Printed in the United States of America.
10 9 8 7 6 5 4 3 2 1

Designed by Scott Piehl.

For Peter. —M. S.

To my son, David. Also, thanks to the
Schmooks, Mrs. Conlon and the kids
at Thomson Estates Elementary,
and my friend Donna. —G. P.

Contents

1

Joshua, sit down in your chair and finish your dinner this minute!"

Josh was in big trouble. He knew he'd be in even bigger trouble if he didn't stop acting up and sit down. But once he started being crazy, he just couldn't stop.

"Joshua," he said, imitating his mother,

"sit down in your chair and finish your dinner this minute!" Josh tried to wag his finger in the air like his mother, but he couldn't quit giggling and rolling his eyes.

"Mommy, what's wrong with Josh?" asked Lizzie, Josh's little sister.

"Do *not* imitate your mother, young man!" said Josh's father.

"Do *not* imitate your mother, young man!" Josh repeated in his dad's voice. Then he laughed very loudly, and Lizzie laughed, too.

Josh's parents weren't laughing. "That's it!" said his father. "Go to your room!"

Josh giggled wildly and swung his arms. One arm hit his glass, and milk splashed across the table and onto his mother.

Josh's mom yelled. His father stood up.

Josh ran laughing to his room and

slammed the door behind him. He paced around, kicking toys and throwing clothes on the floor. He wanted to sit down and catch his breath, but he was too excited. At last, he flopped onto his bed. He wished he could finish his dinner.

He could hear his parents' voices. He was sure they were talking about him. They were probably explaining to Lizzie why her big brother was so weird. Josh wished they would explain it to him, too.

Josh's heart pounded. He tapped his foot against his dresser. Sometimes doing the same thing like that over and over helped him stay in one place and catch his breath.

Someone knocked on his door. "May I come in?" his father asked.

"Pooka-pooka!" said Josh. *Pooka* was his new made-up word today.

"Can you give me a straight answer?" said his father.

"Pooka, yes!" said Josh.

His dad came in and sat on the edge of the bed. "Why do you act like that?"

"I don't know," said Josh.

"Why can't you just sit still at the table like Lizzie? She's only six. You're two years older. I expect you to be the big boy of the family."

Josh hated it when his father compared him to his little sister.

"Do you want to come out and try again?"

"Oh, yes! Pooka-pooka, yes!" said Josh, leaping up from his bed.

2

The next morning, Josh couldn't wait
to get to school. It was Thursday,
his favorite day of the week. On
Thursdays, Josh's class went to the
computer room, and Josh loved computers.
He raced through the house, trying to
find his homework and books and lunchbox.

Except that he kept forgetting what he was supposed to be doing.

"Josh, brush your teeth," his mother reminded him for the third time.

Josh zipped toward the bathroom chanting, "Computer day! Computer day! Computer day! Computer day!"

"I hate computers," said Lizzie, sticking her nose in the air. She was ready to leave for school and stood waiting by the front door with her backpack and lunchbox.

"Josh, is your homework in your backpack?" his mother asked.

"Oh, what do *you* know?" Josh said to Lizzie. "Last week I made a really cool picture on the computer."

"Great," said Josh's mother, "but you have to get your shoes on and—"

"Now they have Geomath. It's a

math and geography game combined."

"Josh," said his mother, "if you don't hurry, you'll get another tardy slip."

"All right! All right!" said Josh. "Why is everybody always bugging me?" He stalked into the bathroom and slammed the door.

Halfway to school, Josh remembered that he had left his homework on the dining room table.

3

Josh's teacher, Mrs. Conrad, was explaining something important, something Josh knew he should hear. But no matter how hard he tried, Josh just couldn't concentrate.

Everything in his classroom distracted

him. Toby Willis tap-tap-tapped his foot like a drum. The clock tick-tock-ticked so loudly Josh couldn't help but check to see how much longer he had to wait until lunchtime. And the chain on the flagpole outside clang-clang-clanged in the wind. All Josh could hear was tapping, ticking, and clanging.

"Josh?" Suddenly, everything was quiet. Mrs. Conrad was looking at him. "Do you know the answer?" she said.

"To what?" Josh asked. He looked around the room. His classmates stared at him. Alex Pitts looked like he was trying hard not to laugh out loud.

"What is ten times fifteen?"

"One hundred and fifty," Josh called out.

Alex stopped grinning, but Danita Rogers said, "Big deal. Everybody knows that.

What's a thousand times a million?"

"A billion," said Josh.

One of the kids said, "Wow!" But math was easy for Josh.

"Very good, Josh," Mrs. Conrad said, smiling.

Josh looked at Alex Pitts, who was grinning at him and making faces. Josh stood up and started to walk toward Alex's desk.

"Josh? Where are you going?" Mrs. Conrad asked.

"Pooka!" Josh answered.

"Please sit down," said Mrs. Conrad.

Josh sank into his seat. At home, at school, it seemed like someone was always telling him to sit down, stop fidgeting, hurry up, or be quiet.

Josh turned around in his seat to face

Tonia Mullins and pretended to stab her arm with one of her pencils.

"Mrs. Conrad," said Tonia, "Josh is bothering me."

"Josh, please face the front of the class and keep your hands to yourself."

"Okay," said Josh.

Alex grinned at him. His lips formed the nickname that Josh hated: *Slosh*.

4

Josh loved and hated the cafeteria. He loved it because he got to talk and laugh with the other kids. But he hated it because it was big and noisy. He couldn't pay attention to anything because he wanted to watch everything.

He watched the men and women serving

food. He watched the tall fifth and sixth graders coming in. Most of all, he watched his classmates making funny faces and laughing.

"Josh, eat your lunch," said a teacher as she passed by his table. But Josh was too excited to eat, and his stomach felt tight. He wished he could leave the lunchroom and go out onto the playground. Things were so much less noisy there, and Josh could find places where he could be alone for a few minutes to calm down.

Before he realized what he was doing, Josh started pulling on the jacket of Dan Jacobs, the boy next to him.

"Stop it," said Dan, but Josh didn't stop. He wished he could stop, but he just pulled harder on Dan's jacket. Finally, Dan yelled so loudly that the teacher came back to where they were sitting.

"Make him quit bothering me!" said Dan.

"Stop bothering Dan," the teacher told Josh.

Josh made a wild face.

"Josh, I think you'd better take a five-minute time-out. Then I want you to go outside and play."

Time-outs always made Josh feel terrible. Sitting all alone during lunch time embarrassed him. He was angry with the teacher for putting him by himself. But mostly he was angry with himself because he couldn't stay out of trouble.

On the way outside after his time-out, Josh realized that he hadn't even gotten around to eating his lunch.

On the playground, Toby and Alex were kicking the soccer ball around. Josh ran to

join them. He loved soccer.

"Want to play, Josh?" Toby said.

"You can have him," said Alex. "No Slosh on my team."

"Why not?" said Toby. "Josh is the best soccer player in our class."

Good old Toby, thought Josh.

But Alex said, "Slosh? He's a freak. He can't even sit still in class. What a goof. Right, Slosh?"

"Shut up!" said Josh. "Don't call me that."

"Sit down, Josh," said Alex, imitating Mrs. Conrad's voice and snapping his fingers in Josh's face. "Yoohoo, Josh-y, wake up, it's lunchtime!" Alex reached out and shoved Josh's shoulder.

Josh shoved Alex back. "Shut up! Shut up! Shut up!"

"Josh!" said a voice behind him. It was Mrs. Conrad.

"Keep your hands to yourself! You will take a five-minute time-out this instant!"

"But—" Josh started to say.

"Time-out!" said Mrs. Conrad.

y the time his mother picked him up, Josh was furious. He threw his lunchbox and backpack onto the floor of the car.

"I hate school!" he said, sinking down in his seat.

"Another bad day?" his mother said.

"I can't help it," said Josh. "The other kids do it."

"Do what?" said his mother.

"They get me in trouble."

"And how do they do that?"

"Alex Pitts called me Slosh, and I hate that, and when I told him to shut up, Mrs. Conrad heard me and put me in time-out. And Tonia left her pencils out, and I couldn't help but play with them. And all the noises in the classroom got me all distracted so that I couldn't hear what Mrs. Conrad said. And stupid Alex and Toby made faces at me and got me in trouble. And I forgot my homework. And because of all that I had to miss computer class, and that's my favorite class of the whole week, and *I missed it!* I *hate* school!"

Josh pushed back the tears until his cheeks hurt. His mother leaned across the front seat to hug him. She said, "I think it's time we had a talk with your teacher."

Josh's parents went to see Mrs. Conrad the next day after school. Josh ran to see them on the playground after their meeting.

"What did she say?" he asked.

"She said you move around and fidget a lot and you distract your classmates," said his mom.

Josh looked at the ground.

"She also said that the other kids tease you a lot."

So Mrs. Conrad knew! Well, that was good news, anyway.

"Know what else she said?" Josh's father asked. "She said you were one of the

smartest kids in your class—especially in computers and math."

"No way," said Josh.

"Yes way!" said his father.

Josh smiled.

"Mrs. Conrad recommended that you see a special doctor," said Josh's mother.

"What kind of doctor?"

"A doctor who studies the way people think."

"Pooka-pooka!" said Josh. "That's the way I think."

"Yes," said Josh's father. "We know."

6

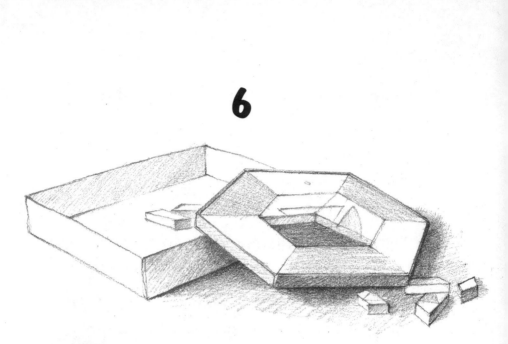

Dr. Hartnett didn't mind that Josh couldn't sit still or that he walked around touching everything in her office.

After Josh's parents left, the doctor talked to Josh. She gave him some puzzles and watched while he solved them. When he was done, Dr. Hartnett said, "Good work, Josh!" Then she asked him some questions.

Her voice was soft.

"You know, Josh, I think I might be able to help you," Dr. Hartnett said. "Some kids have a problem that keeps them from being able to pay attention. It's called ADD."

"Add?" said Josh.

"Not like addition," said Dr. Hartnett. "A-D-D. It stands for Attention Deficit Disorder. A lot of kids have ADD. Some of them are also what we call hyperactive."

"Is that like when my mom says I'm too 'hyper'?" Josh asked.

Dr. Hartnett nodded. "Kind of. People who are hyperactive have a very hard time being still. They have to move around and fidget a lot. Do you ever do those things?"

"Yeah, all the time," said Josh.

"I bet that makes your teacher angry."

Josh nodded. "And my parents."

Dr. Hartnett smiled. "Does your mind wander when you don't want it to?"

"Yeah!" said Josh. "How did you know that?"

"Because that's how ADD is. People with ADD have trouble concentrating. Children and adults, too. And when people can't pay attention and they need to move around a lot, we say they have Attention Deficit with Hyperactivity, or ADHD. That might be what you have."

Josh had a question, but before he could ask it, Dr. Hartnett said, "I bet you want to know if you'll always have ADD."

"Will I?" Josh asked.

"Maybe. But for lots of people, it starts to go away as they get older. That's what happened to me."

"Really?" Josh said. "You had it, too?"

He couldn't believe it. Dr. Hartnett was so calm.

"Yep! I had exactly the same problems that you're having now. I was lucky because I had parents like yours who wanted to help me."

"What if it doesn't go away as I get older?" Josh asked.

"Well," said Dr. Hartnett, "there are lots of ways that we can help you to remember to concentrate—now and as you get older. We're all going to work together—you, me, your parents, and your teacher—to help you do your best in school and at home."

"Like a team?" Josh asked.

"Exactly like a team!" said Dr. Hartnett.

7

That night at dinner, Josh's mother said, "Dr. Hartnett was nice, wasn't she?"

"Really nice," said Josh.

"Josh, are you sick?" asked Lizzie.

"Yeah! Really sick!" Josh jumped straight up from his seat, bumping the table hard. He grabbed his throat and stuck out his tongue. Lizzie giggled and clapped.

"Josh, sit down," said his mother. But Josh kept making faces at Lizzie, and Lizzie kept laughing. "Joshua, sit down," his mother said again, quietly. This time Josh sat.

"We talked to the doctor for a while, too," said Josh's father. "She gave us some good advice. We're going to meet with Dr. Hartnett and your teacher to see if we can work together to help you in school."

"Cool!" said Josh.

"I think we're also going to start a token system," said Josh's mother.

"A what?" said Josh.

Josh's father explained. "We agree on how you can earn stickers to help you remember what you have to do."

"Like sit down in my seat?" Josh asked.

"For starters," said his mother. "Or getting ready in the morning without being reminded twenty times."

"Then, when you've filled up your chart with stickers, you can trade it in for something cool," his father said.

"I want to earn stickers, too," said Lizzie.

"Okay," said her father. "You can, too."

"So can I have my first sticker?" said Josh, jumping up from his chair.

"Not so fast, buster," said his mother. "You have to sit there through dinner. I think you can do it!"

"Me, too!" said his father.

"Me, too!" said Josh, and he did.

8

After that, things began to change for Josh. For one thing, Mrs. Conrad moved Josh's chair to the front of the room. Josh liked it much better at the front. He wasn't distracted by the other kids as much, and he could hear Mrs. Conrad better. Sometimes when he still got distracted, Mrs. Conrad would touch him on the shoulder. This helped remind him that he needed to calm down and pay attention.

Mrs. Conrad started a sticker chart at school, too. The first week, Josh earned lots of stickers. But sometimes he lost stickers. Once he talked too loudly after Mrs. Conrad warned him twice. Another time, he pulled up his shirt in music class to make Emily Dalhart laugh. Even so, by the end of the week, he had earned twenty-three stickers and almost finished his chart.

The second week was even better. He earned thirty stickers. His father told him how proud he was and took Josh to the toy store on Saturday to trade in his sticker chart for a baseball cap. Josh had lots of caps, but he was proudest of this one because he had earned it himself.

Josh wished he didn't have ADD, but

he felt better knowing there was a reason why he sometimes couldn't sit still or pay attention when he wanted to. Just knowing that made it easier to concentrate. The more he paid attention, the less he bothered people. And the less he bothered them, the nicer they were to him.

But there still were times when Josh had trouble paying attention. Sometimes all he could hear was ticking, tapping, rustling, even breathing. Then all the stickers in the world couldn't keep him in his seat when school got boring. And once, when he threw an eraser at Alex, he lost three stickers and had to spend fifteen minutes in time-out.

9

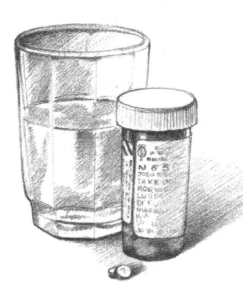

ne day after school, Josh's parents, Dr. Hartnett, and Mrs. Conrad all met together. They talked about Josh and how to help him pay attention better. Dr. Hartnett gave them some tips and said she wanted to see Josh in her office.

The next time he and his parents went to see Dr. Hartnett, she suggested that Josh try medicine for his ADHD.

"But I don't want to take pills," said Josh. "I don't feel sick."

Josh's mother laughed. "I don't think someone who eats three peanut butter sandwiches every day could be very sick."

"People take medicine for all sorts of reasons," Dr. Hartnett explained. "Not just when they're sick."

"How often will he have to take the medicine?" Josh's father asked.

"We're going to start Josh on a very low dosage once a day. Josh's teacher tells me he has trouble settling down in the morning. I think he might need just a little help. As he grows and his body gets bigger, he might need more medicine, but then again, maybe not. We'll just have to see how it goes."

"No! No pills!" said Josh.

"Josh, tell me something," said Dr. Hartnett. "If you couldn't see well, you'd want to wear glasses, right?"

"Maybe," said Josh.

"This medicine will be like that for you. But instead of helping you to see better, it might help you to listen and pay attention better in school. It might help you to filter out the distractions you told me about."

"You'd like that, wouldn't you?" Josh's mother asked him.

"I guess so," said Josh.

"Tell you what," said Dr. Hartnett. "Why don't you try it for a few days, then come

back and see me. If it doesn't help, we'll talk about what to do. If it makes you feel bad, tell your parents right away, and we'll try something else. Deal?" Dr. Hartnett held out her hand.

"Deal," said Josh, and they shook hands.

10

As it turned out, Dr. Hartnett was right—the medicine did help. The day he took his first pill, Josh sat at his desk listening to Mrs. Conrad. She was explaining the multiplication exercise they were about to do.

Alex was making goofy faces at Josh, trying to get him distracted. But for once, that didn't bother Josh. He hoped he would be the one Mrs. Conrad picked to solve the math problem.

Mrs. Conrad looked at Dan Jacobs. "Dan," she said, "could you please stop tapping your foot? It's very distracting."

Wow! thought Josh. He hadn't even heard Dan tapping his foot on the leg of his desk. And he had heard every word of what Mrs. Conrad had said. It felt great to hear what she said!

"Now," said Mrs. Conrad, "who wants to solve a problem?"

Josh's hand shot straight up in the air.

Later, in the cafeteria, Josh ate all his lunch without any of the teachers having to speak to him. The noise and bustle of the

cafeteria didn't give him a nervous
feeling like it usually did. Josh wondered
if that was because of the medicine.

After lunch, Toby and Josh ran to the
playground with Josh's soccer ball. Alex
was already there with Dan.

"Want to play soccer?" Toby asked Alex
and Dan.

"Sure, but I call 'no Slosh,'" said Dan.

Josh suddenly realized that no one had
called him Slosh in a long time. He had
forgotten how bad that name made him
feel.

Alex spoke up. "His name is not Slosh.
It's Josh. And Josh is the best soccer player
in our class, and he's on my team. Okay?"

"Sure," said Dan. "Whatever."

Josh couldn't believe his ears. Was Alex
Pitts really standing up for him?

Alex just grinned and said, "Okay, Josh.
Are you ready to play?"

Josh couldn't help but grin, too. "Yep!"
he said, "I'm ready!"

And he was.